MW00961212

WITHDRAWN

Groundwood Books / House of Anansi Press
groundwoodbooks.com

We acknowledge for their financial support of our publishing program the Canada
Council for the Arts, the Ontario Arts Council and the Government of Canada.

Canada Council   Conseil des Arts
for the Arts   du Canada

ONTARIO ARTS COUNCIL
CONSEIL DES ARTS DE L'ONTARIO
an Ontario government agency
un organisme du gouvernement de l'Ontario

With the participation of the Government of Canada
Avec la participation du gouvernement du Canada | Canadä

Library and Archives Canada Cataloguing in Publication
Beam, Matt, author
The zombie prince / Matt Beam ; [illustrated by] Luc Melanson.
Issued in print and electronic formats.
ISBN 978-1-55498-997-3 (hardcover). – ISBN 978-1-55498-998-0 (PDF)
I. Melanson, Luc, illustrator II. Title.
PS8603.E352Z36 2018   jC813'.6   C2018-900051-1
C2018-900052-X

The illustrations were done digitally.
Design by Michael Solomon
Printed and bound in Malaysia

MIX
Paper from
responsible sources
FSC® C012700
FSC
www.fsc.org

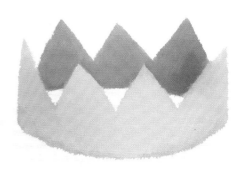

To Emile and Iris.
MB

To Marie-Claude.
LM

the ZOMBiE PRiNCE

Matt Beam   pictures by Luc Melanson

Groundwood Books
House of Anansi Press
Toronto   Berkeley

Brandon is a zombie who will destroy his enemies with the tears falling down his face.

The only people who aren't his enemies, he says,
are Oscar, who is lying beside him on the school
lawn, Ms. Gomez, who said fairies are fearless
creatures, and me.

I am sitting cross-legged at Brandon's feet,
twirling an orange leaf in my fingers.

Oscar sits up suddenly and says he is a ghost.
Next time, he will float invisibly in front of
Brandon and block the mean words sailing
through the air toward him. Oscar spreads out
his arms, drops his head, and for a moment, he
disappears right in front of our eyes.

When he returns, Oscar says, "You don't have that many enemies, though — just Sam."

Brandon's eyes go bright and then dark and then bright again, as a cloud above moves past the sun in a hurry.

"I'm not so sure," he replies finally.

"I am a vampire, then," I declare, turning up my blue collar. "But instead of sucking blood from people's necks, I suck bad things from the air, like pollution and Mrs. Clark's perfume clouds and Sam's mean words. I will suck them all up like a vacuum and make them go away forever. That's why my front tooth is missing. See?"

"Sam was wrong to hurt you with her words," Ms. Gomez said gently at recess, with a hand on Brandon's shoulder. "But it wasn't the flower's fault."

With his ghostly hands, Oscar pulls up grass and dirt, and digs out a resting place for the daisy with no petals and a bent stem.

When the flower finally disappears into the ground, I poke the sole of my best friend's shoe.

"Sam *was* wrong, Brandon,"
I say. "I mean, you'd make an
awesome fairy, but you actually
looked more like a prince."

"A zombie prince," Oscar declares
triumphantly, jumping to his feet. But then
he shakes his head. "I don't think you can
destroy your enemies with your tears, though.
It doesn't work that way."

Brandon's arms are now behind his head,
and the trails from his tears are almost dry on
his freckled cheeks.

"Yeah," he says finally. "A zombie prince —
I like that."

Oscar makes wing tips of his dirty hands
and airplanes away toward the water
fountain.

"Check out those clouds up there," Brandon says to me, pointing up to the sky. "They look like baby yetis."

I squint up toward the clouds, blocking the sun with the palm of my hand. Its rays shoot through my fingers like magical laser beams.

The clouds just look like clouds to me, though. I turn back to say this when I see that Brandon's eyes are closed.

And he is smiling.